L349f

FOX UNDER FIRST BASE

For Grania, Liam, Siobhán, and Brendan
—*J. L.*

To Paige
All my thanks and love
—*Lisa*

Charles Scribner's Sons Books for Young Readers
Macmillan Publishing Company • 866 Third Avenue, New York, New York 10022
Collier Macmillan Canada, Inc.
1200 Eglinton Avenue East, Suite 200, Don Mills, Ontario M3C 3N1

Printed in the United States of America by Horowitz Rae
First Edition   10   9   8   7   6   5   4   3   2   1

Library of Congress Cataloging-in-Publication Data
Latimer, Jim, 1943–
Fox under first base / Jim Latimer ;
pictures by Lisa McCue. —1st ed.   p.   cm.
Summary: A baseball-stealing fox makes reparation and is duly rewarded.
[1. Animals—Fiction.   2. Baseball—Fiction.]   I. McCue, Lisa, ill.   II. Title.
PZ7.L369617Fo   1991   [E]—dc20   89-27576   CIP   AC
ISBN 0-684-19053-2

The author and publishers gratefully acknowledge
the kind assistance of Mr. Peter Clark, registrar of the
National Baseball Hall of Fame and Museum at Cooperstown, New York.

FOX UNDER FIRST BASE

JIM LATIMER · Pictures by LISA McCUE

CHARLES SCRIBNER'S SONS · NEW YORK

Collier Macmillan Canada · Toronto
Maxwell Macmillan International Publishing Group
New York · Oxford · Singapore · Sydney

Getting fat for fall was a lot of work.

It was September, almost fall. James Bear had been in the tall grass, grazing all day, all week. Grazing his whole life, he almost thought. James's teeth ached. His cheeks and tongue ached. There were stems and chaff clinging to his coat and ears.

James stopped grazing. He gave his coat a shake, spraying stems in every direction. He stood in the sunshine, warm air hopping in his ears. James thought about shade. He thought about his friend Skunk, who was a great collector. Skunk's name was Laurel. She lived in the forest, in a cool clearing, a place filled with shade and found objects—fountain pens and clock springs and a colored parachute.

Bear decided he would visit his friend Skunk. He would give his teeth a rest. With relief and a sigh, James Bear turned his back on the tall grass and lumbered off toward the forest.

At the forest's edge, a little beyond, James found a tree with shade. He sat down with his back to the tree, his forepaws looking like huge plates beside him. He would rest here for one minute, he decided. James sat resting his teeth and his eyes—for about one minute. Until he felt a paw on his paw.

The paw tapped.

Bear blinked.

The eyes of a gray fox, his nose almost touching Bear's, were staring from behind square, steel-framed glasses.

"Bear?" said the fox.

"Fox?" Bear answered him.

"I didn't want to wake you," said the fox, pushing his glasses up the bridge of his nose. The gray fox looked away for a moment, apparently reconsidering, and then looked back. "I did want to wake you," he admitted, "because you look friendly. I have never been in this forest before."

It was no trouble being wakened, Bear told him. James Bear explained that he had been eating alfalfa, getting fat. He was glad to have someone to talk to.

Fox's proper name was Gerald. Like Skunk and Bear, though, he rarely used his name. Fox pushed his square-lensed glasses to the top of his nose. "Look," he said.

Bear looked. Fox handed him a round, white object that he could not identify. Bear held the thing in his paws. It was a ball, as white as a starched collar, its seam stitched with red yarn in a herringbone pattern. It was lovely.

"Lovely," said Bear.

"You may have it," said Fox. "It is a baseball. I am a collector." Fox told Bear he could have the ball for one day.

Bear thanked him. Fox, waving, disappeared into the forest.

James Bear sat, turning the stitched, starched-white ball in his paws, wondering what it might be for. He brushed an alfalfa stem from his fur and yawned. The shadows seemed to lengthen and deepen around him. He closed his eyes. Bear began to drift and dream, until he felt a paw, a second paw, this time on his shoulder.

The paw tapped.

Bear blinked awake and stared into the eyes of a muffled porcupine.

The porcupine was wearing a checked muffler and a belt with handcuffs. She smelled sharply of menthol and eucalyptus. The porcupine coughed behind her paw. "I beg your pardon," she said. "My name is Detective Chief Inspector Porcupine."

Bear blinked.

"A police officer," Porcupine explained.

"My name is Bear," Bear told her, hoping he had not done something illegal. The detective chief inspector asked whether Bear would object to answering a question—maybe several, depending on his answers. Bear said he would try, and the detective offered him a throat lozenge, slipping one into her own mouth and swallowing it almost at once.

"Would you have seen a fox, by any chance?" the porcupine detective asked.

Instinctively, Bear covered Fox's baseball with his paw. "How do you mean 'seen a fox'?" he answered.

"A sort of grayish fox," said Porcupine, "possibly with a ball, white with red stitches."

"A grayish fox with a ball?" Bear asked her. He wondered what Gray Fox had done, and nearly asked, but the detective chief inspector interrupted him.

"His name is Gerald," she explained, "though he is now known as The Fox Under First Base." Porcupine paused and sneezed into her handkerchief. "Because he has tunneled under the ballpark," she told Bear. "We have traced him there. He actually lives under first base."

James Bear's expression was blank. He was altogether puzzled. He had never seen a ballpark. He had never heard of first base.

The porcupine detective chief inspector sighed and swallowed a lozenge and tried to explain these things.

"Baseball," she began, "is a sport. It is a game," Porcupine said, "though it is quite serious. Baseball is mostly played by birds. Blue jays and orioles and cardinals. Tigers also play, though—and giants." Porcupine paused for a breath. "Now, the game of baseball," she continued, "is played in a park, called a stadium, on a chalked square, called a diamond. A chalked square with cushions, called bases, at the corners, though in one corner there is a plate, and in the center there is a *rubber* made of rock." Porcupine paused again. "Fox," she resumed, "actually lives under one of these cushions, the one called first base. Now," Porcupine continued, throwing the tails of her muffler over her shoulders, "the object of baseball is first to be safe—I mean to be safe at first, and then second, and then third base—and then to come home."

Bear nodded. "To be safe," he repeated, "and then come home."

Porcupine sighed and sneezed. "Yes," she said, sighing again. "Animals don't realize how difficult detective investigations are."

Bear nodded. "You have to explain a lot."

"Yes," said the chief inspector. "Report and explain. Track animals into odd places. Follow them at all times of day and night and in all types of weather, often catching cold. Are you sure you wouldn't like a cough drop?"

Bear accepted a lozenge and thanked Porcupine.

"Well," she concluded, "I'll be on my way. Thank you, Bear, for your cooperation."

Bear gave Porcupine a wave, lifting his paw, uncovering Fox's baseball.

"THERE," shouted the detective inspector. She had noticed the ball. "There is a white, stitched ball—a baseball. A perfect example. So you will have no trouble recognizing one," she said. "The ballpark is missing one hundred baseballs."

Porcupine tossed the tails of her muffler over her shoulders and returned Bear's wave. "Thank you again," she said, and continued on her way.

The moment Porcupine disappeared from sight, Bear set out in search of The Fox Under First Base.

When Bear found him, the gray fox was sitting beside a marshy pond, watching bumblebees. The late-afternoon sun was glinting on the frames of Fox's glasses. The bumblebees, foraging for pollen in the goldenrod, were paying no attention to him.

Fox brightened when he saw Bear. "Bear," he said, "how are you enjoying your ball?"

Bear sat down beside the fox. "Fox," he said, looking very grave, ignoring Fox's question.

"What?" Fox answered, peering at Bear from behind his glasses.

But something else had suddenly captured Bear's attention, distracting him from Fox. He was staring over Fox's shoulder.

"What?" said Fox again.

"There," said Bear, pointing to a gap in the brush.

Fox turned and peered toward the place Bear was pointing to. There was a porcupine, muffled almost to her teeth and walking, watching the ground, as if she might be tracking someone. Someone or some*thing*.

"That is a detective inspector, a police officer," said Bear. "She's looking for The Fox Under First Base."

Fox's eyes widened behind his glasses. Porcupine, still tracking, was closer now, coming nearer. Her muffled cough was almost audible.

"What do you want to do?" Bear whispered to Fox. Porcupine, quite close now, coughed and sneezed. Fox gave Bear a look.

"I'd like to run," he said.

Bear rose to his feet.

Fox jumped to his feet.

Together, like lightning and thunder, like shots from a cannon, Fox and Bear exploded into motion.

James was fast, wonderfully fast for an animal with fire-hydrant feet and dinner-plate paws. He ran with a rolling gait, galloping with his ears laid back, his tail tucked in. Fox was fast, too. He was a gray streak, a blur beside Bear. And yet, fast though they were, there were factors tending to slow both Fox and Bear down today. Bear, growing fat, preparing for fall and winter, was burdened by his weight. Fox's short-sightedness and his slipping-down glasses slowed him a little.

The two animals, one heavy, one shortsighted, crashed through the forest together, breaking branches as they ran, rolling over shrubs and trees, making a wreck of the woods. Fox and Bear ran that way for a short time, for about five minutes, and then stopped, breathless, to rest. Moments later, muffled to her teeth, coughing her cough, still tracking, watching the ground, Porcupine came into view again.

Could she have followed so fast? Bear wondered. He didn't see how she could have. And yet there was her cough. There was her checked muffler. Maybe he and Fox had run in a circle. Or maybe this was the fastest-tracking porcupine detective chief inspector in the world.

Fox was frightened now, Bear saw. "Don't worry," he said, pushing Fox behind him, and then Porcupine walked up.

"Bear," she said, almost shouted. Porcupine looked to her left, then to her right, then behind her. "*Wasn't* there a fox?" she said, and sneezed. "I was sure I was tracking a fox." Porcupine looked puzzled. "Of course," she said, "I can't *smell*." She sneezed again. "But there were fox footprints—and a bear's beside them. I was tracking a fox and a bear, I thought."

"It is a lot of work, being a detective," Bear offered.

Porcupine sighed, almost sneezed. "You are right," she said. The detective chief inspector squinted at the fox footprints and bear footprints, now mingled with her own porcupine prints. She sniffed at them halfheartedly. Porcupine sighed again, straightening. "Well, Bear," she said, "it was good to see you again. Have you got your ball?"

Bear showed her his ball.

"Good," she told him. "Well," Porcupine continued, "if you see The Fox Under First Base, tell him we're looking for him. Tell him the police are looking for him."

Bear said he would.

When Porcupine had gone, Bear turned to Fox and gave him a long look. "How many baseballs do you have?" he asked.

Fox looked away. He pushed his glasses to the bridge of his nose, then looked back at Bear. "One hundred," he admitted.

"You are The Fox Under First Base, aren't you?" Bear said.

Fox looked away.

"Fox," Bear said, "you must give them back."

"Why?" asked Fox.

Bear thought a moment. "I don't know how to explain," he said. "Because . . . because the players, the baseball players, want to be safe." Bear thought again. "To be safe," he said, "and then to come home."

Fox nodded sadly. "I will give them back," he told Bear.

Fox returned one hundred baseballs, scattering them into play one at a time from his hiding place under first base. The ballplayers, coaches, and umpires were confused by this at first. But gradually they grew accustomed to it. After one week all one hundred baseballs were returned.

When Fox came back to Bear's woods, his ears were drooping. His glasses had slipped to the end of his nose, and he let them stay there. Bear called out a lively greeting when they met.

"Fox," he called, "it's good to see you."

"Hello, Bear," said Fox, looking very gloomy.

"Did you give them back?" Bear asked him, hoping he had.

Fox nodded.

"*All* of them?" asked Bear.

Fox nodded.

"How do you feel?" asked Bear.

Fox peered over the rims of his glasses. "I feel awful," he said.

Bear put a paw on Fox's shoulder. "Well," he told Fox, "come with me. I have something to show you. There is someone who wants to meet you." Fox adjusted his glasses and went with Bear.

James Bear shepherded his friend—for now Fox was a friend—to a rock above a clearing, Skunk's clearing. They stopped a moment to survey Skunk's collection: corkscrews and clock springs and skeleton keys. Picture frames, broken bells, and pencil leads. And a radiator and a parachute.

Fox's eyes widened. Skunk's radiator, freshly painted, gleamed in the September sunshine. Her parachute, orange and purple, green and black, was spread out to its full dimensions. Skunk was fixing a seam with needle and thread. Bear called down to her, introducing Fox. The two of them climbed down together.

Fox admired Skunk's keys and clock springs and her bottle caps, but when Bear showed him Skunk's collection of mechanical pencils, Fox was speechless.

There were pencils painted navy blue and fire-engine red; pencils made of rosewood and tortoiseshell; pencils with fittings made of silver and nickel and brass; pencils with tiny figures engraved on them, trout flies and moose heads. Fox adjusted his glasses and narrowed his eyes. There was a pencil with a tiny herringbone design, like the seam of a baseball.

Fox's eyes went out of focus. His glasses slipped down. The herringbone pencil reminded him of his baseballs. He was not going to stop thinking about them. He was not going to stop missing them. When Fox's eyes focused again, he found he was staring at a stitched ball.

Skunk was holding in her paws a yellowed baseball, threadbare and faded, with scratches and smudged writing on its cover. Fox adjusted his glasses.

"How many stitches are there in the cover of a baseball, did you say?" Skunk asked.

Fox hadn't said. "In the modern, major-league baseball, there are one hundred eight stitches," he told Skunk. Fox was still staring at the scuffed ball. "I don't know how many there are in a very old baseball."

"In this one there are one hundred sixteen," Skunk told him. "I have counted them. It was signed by a player without shoes," she added.

Fox held Skunk's old baseball in his paws. It was more closely sewn than any he had ever seen. The name *Shoeless Joe* was written on it in smudged ink. Shoeless Joe Jackson. Shoeless Joe was a major-league ball-player, Fox told Bear. He had played for the Chicago White Sox in 1919 when they had almost won—should have won—the World Series. Fox told Skunk that Shoeless Joe had been a wonderful hitter, maybe his favorite, maybe the best.

"You may have the ball," Skunk said.

Fox stared at her. He stared at Bear, then at the ball autographed by Shoeless Joe. "Thank you," he said. Fox asked whether Bear and Skunk wanted to hear the story of the 1919 World Series, Chicago against Cincinnati.

Skunk and Bear said they would like to hear it and listened for the rest of that day to Fox's stories about the 1919 Chicago White Sox and about the grace and power of Shoeless Joe Jackson. When he had finished, shadows were lengthening across Skunk's clearing. Fox told Skunk and Bear they were baseball fans now. Best friends and baseball fans for life.